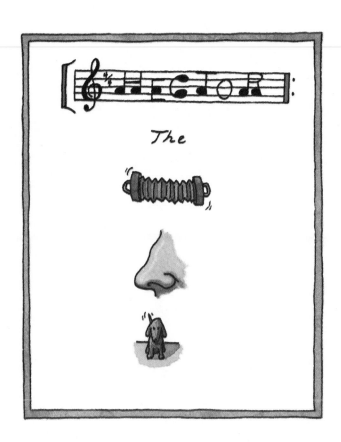

HECTOR

The Accordion-nosed Dog
by John Stadler

BRADBURY PRESS / SCARSDALE, NEW YORK

Manufactured in the United States of America.
3 2 1
The illustrations are full color pen and ink and watercolor paintings,
reproduced in halftone.
Hector, The Accordion-nosed Dog is available in a hardcover edition,
also published by Bradbury Press.
Library of Congress Cataloging in Publication Data
Stadler, John. Hector, the accordion-nosed dog.
Summary: Hector abandons his career as a pointer
for one as a musician when he accidently acquires
an accordion nose.
[1. Dogs—Fiction.   2. Accordion—Fiction]
I. Title.
PZ7. S7756He   [E]   81-7713
                                              AACR2
ISBN 0-02-786680-7

ISBN 0-02-045250-0 (pbk.)

To Karin and Ellen
and to all the Baukhols of Vinstra, Norway

As a boy, Hector lived quietly in the mountains. But once at school, he was found to have an outstanding talent and his life began to change. At graduation, Professor Sludge presented him with the Peabody trophy, the highest honor for excellence in pointing.

Professor Sludge insisted that Hector demonstrate his pointing technique for the eager gathering of parents and teachers.

"Now watch his nose, folks," the professor said as Hector prepared himself.

Hector was all concentration. He tensed his body and sniffed the air. Suddenly, he pointed with his finger and nose to a fly on a rabbit's ear over one mile away.

"Perfect form!" called out one spectator.

"And how well he uses his nose," added another. Hector blushed.

Competing in the Olympic Games, Hector won
eleven gold medals. An all-time record!

"What form! What a nose!" the sportscasters said
again and again.

Hector was an overnight sensation and his life
became a whirlwind. He starred in several TV
commercials, and even made a movie.

Hector moved into a spacious townhouse in the heart
of the city.

"This is the life!" he said.

He was fast . . .

. . . and dashing . . .

. . . and everyone wanted to be his friend.

For a long time, Hector spent most nights at his favorite spot, dancing and prancing into the wee hours of the morning.

Early one dawn, as Hector was showing some admirers just how fast he could run, something terrible happened.

He ran squarely and soundly, smack into a wall.

Hector looked as stiff as a poker, but someone
called for a doctor, anyway.

When Hector finally awoke, he was lying in a hospital room that was filled with strange music. Realizing that he was still alive, he shrieked with joy.

"Now hold on there, Hector," the doctor shouted over the loud music. "You've made a remarkable recovery. However, I must tell you that your nose . . . er—well . . . it's turned into an accordion."

"Huh?" Hector said.

Following his release from the hospital, Hector, overwhelmed with despair, went for a walk along the shore.

"I'm finished," he moaned. "With such a weird nose, I'll never point again."

Back home Hector disconnected the phone and
locked his door. He looked through old scrapbooks full
of his past. From time to time he entertained himself
with a tune on his bent, musical nose, but he never
went out. Finally, Hector's landlord threw him out.

"You didn't pay your rent, buster," he yelled, "and
besides—I hate your crummy music!"

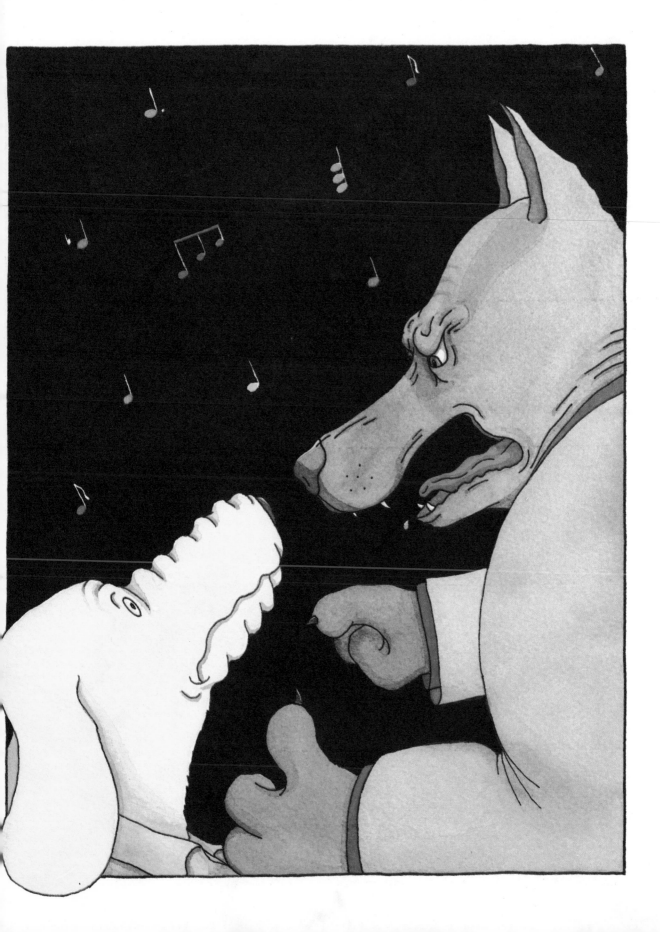

Down and out, Hector walked the streets, wandering aimlessly. Finally he collapsed in a corner, resigned to a life of loneliness and sorrow. "What has become of me?" he sighed.

Bleary-eyed, Hector played a sad, old blues tune.

Hector lost himself in the music. He closed his
eyes and played a beautiful Bach toccata. When he had
finished, standing before him was a crowd tossing
money and cheering, "Bravo! Bravo!"

Hector bowed gratefully and then played a
Gershwin tune, a little Duke Ellington ditty, and ended
with an original composition. The crowd loved it!

Suddenly a figure streaked forward, shouting,
"I am a musical talent agent. Sign here and you will
perform at Canine Hall tonight!"

That evening Hector received a standing ovation from the packed house. "My nose and I are back on top," he thought, "but this time life will be different."

After the show, the lovely opera singer, Miss Lilly deLight (who was starring next-door as Brümhilda in "Die Zaubernüsse") visited Hector in his dressing room to congratulate him. It was love at first sight.

Once again Hector was an overnight sensation. But he and Lilly left the city and made most of their music in the mountains.